Winnie
Shapes Up

For Ina – K.P.

For my very good friend Dianne Bogumsky, with love – xx

OXFORD
UNIVERSITY PRESS

Great Clarendon Street, Oxford OX2 6DP

Oxford University Press is a department of the University of Oxford.
It furthers the University's objective of excellence in research, scholarship,
and education by publishing worldwide in

Oxford New York

Auckland Cape Town Dar es Salaam Hong Kong Karachi
Kuala Lumpur Madrid Melbourne Mexico City Nairobi
New Delhi Shanghai Taipei Toronto

With offices in
Argentina Austria Brazil Chile Czech Republic France Greece
Guatemala Hungary Italy Japan Poland Portugal Singapore
South Korea Switzerland Thailand Turkey Ukraine Vietnam

Oxford is a registered trade mark of Oxford University Press
in the UK and in certain other countries

Text © Oxford University Press 2011
Illustrations © Korky Paul 2011
The characters in this work are the original creation of Valerie Thomas
who retains copyright in the characters.

First published in 2011

British Library Cataloguing in Publication Data
Data available

ISBN: 978-0-19-272990-3 (paperback)

2 4 6 8 10 9 7 5 3 1

Printed in Great Britain by Cox & Wyman Ltd, Reading, Berkshire

Paper used in the production of this book is a natural, recyclable product made
from wood grown in sustainable forests. The manufacturing process conforms
to the environmental regulations of the country of origin

Laura Owen and Korky Paul

Winnie Shapes Up

OXFORD
UNIVERSITY PRESS

contents

Winnie's
Sat Nav

Winnie
Shapes Up

Ssshh! Winnie

There was only a murmur of polite conversation in the shop ... until Winnie came in, barging her way like a rampaging rhinoceros. **Crash!** She had red spots all over her, and she was scratching at them.

Itch, itch! 'Ooo, I'm as itchy as a witchy in a ditchy full of itching powder!' said Winnie. **Trip! Crump!** She knocked over a display. 'Sorry!' shouted Winnie. There was a queue for the counter, but Winnie shoved to the front.

Itch, scratch! ' 'Scuse me!' she shouted. 'I need just one incy little ingredient so that I can make a pepper gherkin potion to get rid of my rash. I'll be as quick as a lick on a lolly stick, I promise! Mr Shopkeeper, have you got a jar of knobbly pickled gherkins and a chilli pepper or two?'

'Well, really!' huffed Mrs Parmar. 'All this noise is most unnecessary! You should join our sponsored silence at school, Winnie!'

'A sponsored what?' asked Winnie.

'Silence,' said Mrs Parmar pulling a leaflet out of her bag. 'You get people to pay you for every minute that you can keep absolutely quiet.'

'Coo!' said Winnie.

'The money goes to the poorest children in the world,' said Mrs Parmar.

'Double coo like a blooming pair of doves!' said Winnie. 'I'll do that for those poor little ordinaries!'

'Ha! You'll never keep quiet!' said
the shopkeeper. The other customers all
laughed at the idea as well.

'I blooming well will!' humphed
Winnie. 'I can keep quiet for, oh, ever
so long!'

'Do it now, then!' said Mrs Parmar.

'All right!' said Winnie.

'Tee-hee! Ha-ha!' went everybody.
'You just said something!'

'That's not flip-flapping fair!' said
Winnie. 'If you promise me money to be
quiet, then I'll keep as quiet as a fossil with
a gag on, you'll see!'

So they all promised to pay Winnie to
keep quiet, and she hurried home.

'Hey, Wilbur,' said Winnie. 'I'm going
to keep quiet for the poorest little
ordinaries in the world.'

'Me-heow!' wondered Wilbur.

'I will!' said Winnie. **Itch!** 'Now, please help me make that potion, Wilbur. If I can just stop this itching I'll be calm and quiet and make lots of money!'

So Wilbur mashed gherkins **squelch!**— and Winnie bashed peppercorns— **crunch!**—and they popped in the chillis and blitzed it all in a mangle-masher— **bzzzbzzzbzz!**—and out came some green gloop.

Winnie slopped the gloop into her hand
and slapped it all over her face.

'There! Have the spots gone?' asked
Winnie. Wilbur pointed to the mirror.
Winnie looked, and put her hands to her
cheeks. 'Heck, the spots have turned blue!'
Then she gasped and gasped again—

'Ah-ah-tishoo!'

'Meeow?' asked Wilbur.

'I-I-I've got the sn-sn-sneeezes!' wailed Winnie. **'Ah-ah-tishoo!** And blue spots! Something's not right!'

Wilbur went to the computer and clicked the mouse to find the 'symptoms and their causes' website.

Wilbur typed in 'blue spots' and 'sneezes'.

Click! The computer spoke the result.

'These symptoms are indicative of an allergic reaction to a surfeit of pepper.'

14

'Oh, no!' wailed Winnie.

'But that's too late!' wailed Winnie.

'Ah-ah-tishoo. I've got to keep quiet for the sponsored silence! **Ah-ah-tishoo.** Today!'

Wilbur brought Winnie a hot drink of warm parsnip juice.

'**Ah-ah-tishoo.**'

He brought her a hot warty bottle.

'**Ah-ah-tishoo.** Heck in a hankie, nothing . . . **ah-tishoo** . . . is going to work!' said Winnie.

So Wilbur brought Winnie her wand.

'Oh, of course! Silly me!' said Winnie. '**Ah-ah-tishoo. Abracadabra!**'

And instantly, there was a bottle with
a seething pink liquid in it, and a large
spoon. Winnie took a spoonful of pink
stuff, then made a face . . . Then there was
silence. The sneezing had stopped.

'Hoo-blooming-ray!' said Winnie.
Then . . .

Hic! Hic-hic!

'Oh, flipping noodles!' said Winnie.
'Hic! Now I've got hiccups that won't
hic! hic! stop. However am I going to
keep quiet?'

'Blleeugh! Hissss!' went Wilbur
to give Winnie a shock.

'Yikes, Wilbur, you made me jump like
a flea in a frying pan!' But . . . silence . . .
the hiccups had gone.

'Yay!' said Winnie. 'Let's go!'

Down in the school hall everyone looked surprised when Winnie walked in.

'Ooer, with all that hiccup fun I'd forgotten about the spots!' said Winnie.

But the little ordinaries and Winnie all
sat down and put fingers to their lips.

'Now,' said Mrs Parmar. 'We will count
down to absolute silence. Five, four, three,
two, one!'

Silence . . . until, **'Hic!'** went Winnie.

Winnie clamped a hand over her mouth,
but she couldn't hold them in. **Hic! hic!**

'Disqualified!' boomed Mrs Parmar so loudly that Winnie jumped as high as a kangaroo on a trampoline . . . and the hiccups were properly gone!

'Oo, ooo, please let me try again!' said Winnie. 'For the sake of those poor little ordinaries?'

'Oh, I suppose so,' said Mrs Parmar.
'Five, four, three, two, one . . .'

Silence. Tick, tock, tick, tock. Silence
for a minute. Winnie rested her head on
the table. Tick, tock, tick, tock. Silence for
half a minute more . . . then:

Snooooore.
GRUNT!!
Sn-sn-snooore!

'Disqualified!' whispered Mrs Parmar.

Wilbur put his head in his paws.

The little ordinaries kept quiet for minutes and minutes, but then they were beginning to get bored . . . until something wonderful happened. Winnie started to talk her dream . . .

'. . . Wilbur the panther stalks his walk and talks to a teasing monkey in a tree . . . and that monkey is me! And I'm flying on a banana—wheeee! Up to where my wings flip-flap fly me to the big silver moon . . . that's a pool of deep water, and in I dive . . .'

The little ordinaries sat in silence, listening to the mumble of dream as an hour and more passed. The words tumbled and the clock tick-tocked and on Winnie went . . . 'So we make sandwiches of leaves and bugs and pepper, lots of pepper, and I sniff and . . .'

24

Winnie suddenly sat up, looking
startled. **'Ah-ah-ah!'** she went.
'Ah-ah-atishooo!' And off shot her
blue spots . . . to land on Mrs Parmar.

'Ha ha ha!' laughed the little ordinaries.

Brrrrp! went Mrs Parmar's whistle.
'Disqualified, all of you! The sponsored
silence is at an end!' said Mrs Parmar.

'Uh-oh! Was that my flipping fault?' asked Winnie.

'In a way,' said Mrs Parmar. 'But you kept the children beautifully quiet for far longer than they could ever have lasted without your dream story to keep them entertained. The children have raised lots of money, and I thank you for that, Winnie.'

'Oh, goody three shoes,' said Winnie.
'Um. Don't worry about the spots, Mrs P.
They'll be gone in twenty-four hours or
sooner if you have a good sneeze.'

'What spots?' said Mrs Parmar.

But Winnie and Wilbur were already
on their way home.

27

Flipping Winnie

'It's a blooming lovely spring day!' said Winnie, hopping on one leg as she tugged-up a boot lace. 'The sun's shining, grass is growing, flowers are flowering, lambs and funny rabbits are hopping, and . . . er . . . and there's something very strange walking up the drive.' Winnie peered further out of the window.

'Meeow?'

'No, silly me, it's only Mrs Parmar! Whatever in the witchy world does she want?'

29

Snap! 'Oh, my blooming bootlace has broken!'

Winnie shiffle-shuffled to the front door.

'Good morning, Winnie,' said Mrs Parmar. 'Did you know that today is Spring Fair Day?' Mrs Parmar glanced at Winnie's feet. 'They are giving away nice shoes as prizes, you know.'

'Ooo, just what I need!' said Winnie.
'What do I do to win a pair?'

'Well, there's a pancake competition,'
said Mrs Parmar.

'Pancakes?' said Winnie. 'Easy-peasy
squashed-slug squeezy! My cowpat
pancakes are famous!'

Mrs Parmar made a face. 'You'd have to
make a normal kind of pancake for racing.'

31

VA-VROOOOoM!

'Racing?' said Winnie. 'Do the pancakes work as wheels, then?'

'No, no,' said Mrs Parmar. 'You run, holding your frying pan with a pancake in it, and while you run you keep tossing the pancake up into the air so that it flips over and lands on the other side.'

'That's sounds fun!' said Winnie. 'Are you racing, Mrs P?'

32

Mrs Parmar shook her head. 'I've never won any prize in my entire life, so there's really no point.'

'That's as sad as a centipede with sore feet who can't find his soft slippers,' said Winnie. 'So how should I make a *normal* pancake?'

'Plain flour,' said Mrs Parmar. 'Eggs and milk. You mix them all together into a smooth batter, then pour the batter into a pan to cook.'

'Easy-sneezy!' said Winnie. 'See you at the Fair, then, Mrs P!'

Winnie shut the door. 'Right,' she said 'First I must do something about these blooming boots.'

'Meeow?' suggested Wilbur, offering a big jar with long black things curled inside.

'Liquorice laces—perfect!' said Winnie. She threaded two laces in and out of holes, then tied them. 'Brillaramaroodles! Now for the pancakes. What was the first ingredient Mrs P said? Flowers, wasn't it?'

So they went into the garden and collected a whole basket-full of croakuses and snowdrips and daffidoodles.

'We'd better bash them a bit, or they'll never mix properly,' said Winnie. 'Ooo, I almost forgot! Mrs P particularly said "plain flower", so not those frilly daffidoodles. Put those ones on one side, Wilbur.'

Bang-squelch, they pounded the flowers to a greeny-yellowy mush. 'Eggs next,' said Winnie.

Winnie found an old ostrich egg and Wilbur found a tangle of spider eggs. **Crack-splash-mix,** they broke the big egg and threw in the teeny-tiny eggs and mixed them all into the yellow-green mush.

'Now it just needs a splash of milk,' said
Winnie. She took a bottle of old skunk
milk from the fridge, and poured it in.

Wilbur held his nose.

Slop-whisk! 'Is that a "smooth
batter", Wilbur?'

He pointed a claw at the green lumps
floating in the goo.

'Well, it'll have to do,' said Winnie. 'Get that pan hot so that we can cook it.'

Sizzle-stick!

'Blooming heck!' said Winnie. She scraped and scratched at the blobby green pancake. 'At least it isn't runny. Come on, Wilbur, we don't want to miss the race!'

Step went Winnie, **trip-splat!**

'Ouch! Now the blooming mice have eaten these laces!'

Wilbur handed Winnie her wand. *'Abracadabra!'*

And instantly Winnie's boots were laced with skinny snakes. They hissed, and the mice ran off.

'Ready at last!' said Winnie.

They got down to the Spring Fair field just as the pancake-race contestants were lining up.

'Wait for me!' said Winnie, pushing her way in.

Brrrrrp! went the whistle. And they were off!

Some ran, some walked. Winnie ran past the choir conductor. Pancakes were being tossed up-twiddle-down all around her. Winnie was just running past the school dinner lady when . . .

'Meeow!' said Wilbur, and the head teacher bellowed through a megaphone. 'Anyone not tossing their pancake will be disqualified!'

42

'But my pancake is stuck!' shouted
Winnie, 'It won't . . .' Then, **trip-twiddle-
tumble!** Winnie's skinny snake laces had
got bored so they slithered out of the boot
holes. Because she was running, Winnie's
trip made her somersault right over.

43

'See!' she panted, getting herself up onto her feet again. 'I flipped myself AND my pancake!'

'Doesn't count!' shouted the head teacher. 'The pancake must be tossed *out* of the pan!'

'Oh, nits' knickers!' muttered Winnie. She waved her wand. *Abracadabra!*

This time Winnie's pancake *did* jump
out of her pan. Up-up-up-twiddle . . .
but it didn't come down.

'There's a new moon in the sky! A green
one!' said the head teacher. He clasped
his hands together. 'I've discovered a
new moon! They'll call it "Head Teacher
Moon" after me! I'll be famous!' He did
a little dance. 'I can retire!'

The head teacher gazed at the sky, and the race finished . . . and at last, **neeeeeow-flop!** Winnie's pancake fell back down . . . to land—*splat*—right on Mrs Parmar's head.

'Oh, whoopsy!' said Winnie. 'Sorry,
Mrs P!' Winnie stepped forward to take
the pancake off Mrs Parmar's head, but
trip-splat! the boots did it again. 'Oh,
mouldy maggots!' said Winnie. 'Let's get
everything tied up securely once and for
all.' She waved her wand. *Abracadabra!*

47

Instantly there was a whirl of wild
ribbons flying off the hats the children were
wearing for the best bonnet competition.
Winnie's boots were suddenly firmly tied
with a big red ribbon on the left boot,
a green one on her right. Wilbur had a
pink ribbon on his tail. Mrs Parmar had
a yellow ribbon tied under her chin,
securing the pancake firmly to her head.
The head teacher had a purple ribbon on his
megaphone.

48

'What a very strange day!' he said.
'Er . . . ladies and gentlemen, I had better
announce the winner of our best bonnet
competition.' The head teacher looked
towards the children whose ribbonless
bonnets were falling off their heads.
Then he saw Mrs Parmar.

Wilbur had tucked the daffidoodles into
her pancake bonnet. 'Ah, Mrs Parmar!'
said the head teacher. 'A picture of
springtime beauty! You win the shoes!'

'Oh!' simpered Mrs Parmar.

'See, Mrs P?' said Winnie. 'I bet
the only reason you've never won a
competition before is that you've never
entered one, have you?'

'Well, no I haven't,' agreed Mrs Parmar.

'But I think you should have these lovely
shoes, Winnie!'

'I don't need them now!' said Winnie,
pointing to her boots. 'So we're all happy.'

'Mrrrow!' complained Wilbur, who
was fighting to get the big pink ribbon
off his tail!

Winnie's Sat Nav

Winnie and Wilbur had just finished polishing all the cauldrons.

'All done, Wilbur!' said Winnie, having a nice stretch. 'Now we can do whatever we blooming well like!' But just then . . .

Neeeow-crump! Something flew through the window and landed beside Winnie.

'What the hiccuping heck is that?' said Winnie.

It was a message pod.

'Oooer, how modern!' said Winnie.
'I bet Wanda sent it!'

She had. Winnie pushed the button
on the pod, and heard Wanda's shriek
coming out.

'Winnie! Can you hear me?'

'Of course I blooming can!' said
Winnie, holding the pod away from her ear.

'Winnie, you've got to come and see my new abode. Wayne and I have just moved in. It's at Piddling-in-the-Puddle—ever so picturesque. It's so stylish and convenient and hygienic and up-to-the-minute and architect designed. A neat bungalow. Not like your stinky ramshackle old-fashioned mess of a place, Win! Come to tea and see it. Three o'clock. Oh, and you can bring that scraggy old cat of yours if you must.'

'Mrrrow!' said Wilbur.

'You're abso-blooming-lutely right,
Wilbur!' said Winnie. 'That sister of mine
is as rude as a hippopotamus's bottom.
Still, family is family. We'd better go and
see her boring new abode. We should take
a bungalow-warming present with us.'

'Mrrow?' Wilbur shrugged.

'I've no idea,' said Winnie. 'Perhaps a
nice budgie? It would have to match
her colour scheme.'

Pounce-slurp! acted Wilbur.

'Oo, yes, you're right!' said Winnie.
'A budgie wouldn't last five minutes with
that Wayne about the place! Perhaps a
vulture would be better? It could sit on her
television and sing vulture songs. Hmm.'

57

Twang-cuckoo! Twang-cuckoo!

went Winnie's watch.

'Heck, it's two o'cuckoo already! No time to get any blooming present! We must go! Er . . . where is Piddling-in-the-Puddle?' wondered Winnie.

Wilbur flapped out a big map, but . . .

'Put that map away, Wilbur!' said Winnie. 'I'm going to show Wanda that I can be modern, too!' Winnie waved her wand. *Abracadabra!*

Instantly, there was a sat nav box on the table. Winnie stuck the box and wires onto her broom.

'Hop on board, Wilbur!' she said. Then she poked at the sat nav screen.

Bleep! Bloop-blop!

'All set!'

'Meeeow!' Wilbur rolled up his map and stuck it under his arm.

'We won't need *that*!' scoffed Winnie. 'Sat navs work like magic! Close your eyes and it'll take us where we want to go!'

So Winnie and Wilbur both closed their eyes tight.

'Go!' said Winnie, and whoosh! Up and off they flew.

'Wheeee!' said Winnie.

But soon—**clatter clatter**— Wilbur's teeth were chattering.

'It's b-b-bloooming c-c-cold,' said Winnie. 'I w-w-wonder . . .?' She opened her eyes. 'Heck in a helmet, Wilbur! Look at all those stars! We're *lost*! In *outer space!*'

'Mrrrww!' said Wilbur, pointing a claw.
Just ahead of them was a spaceship with
a big net dangling from it.

'Space fishing!' said Winnie. 'Who?
What?' But she didn't have time to
wonder any more because the spaceship's
net suddenly swooped around Winnie and
Wilbur and the broom.

'Ooeer!' said Winnie as they were
swept up in the net, tumbled through
the door of the spaceship and onto
the floor.

'Well!' said Winnie, untangling herself,
jumping to her feet and wagging a finger.
'Just what . . . Oh!' Winnie suddenly saw
who she was talking to.

Aliens. Lots of aliens.

'Oh. Er . . . hello,' said Winnie.

'Ploot pling pluggle!' said one alien. It pointed at Winnie. Then all the other aliens pointed at her, and they laughed. **'Pli-pli-pli!'**

Then the aliens prodded Winnie.

'Oi!' said Winnie, and she hopped to one side.

'Pli-pli-pli!' laughed the aliens.
They prodded her again until she was
jumping all over the place. The aliens were
so busy laughing that they didn't notice
Wilbur slink and prowl his way around
the edge of the spaceship until he came
to the controls.

Wilbur unfurled his map. Then he began to poke at screens and pull levers and push buttons until—**lurch! swerve!**—the spaceship was suddenly whizzing through space, heading towards Earth.

66

Neeeeeoow-bump! They landed.

'Pliggle?' said the aliens to each other.

'Where are we?' asked Winnie.

Wilbur pointed.

'Wanda's blooming bungalow!' said
Winnie. 'And there she is!'

'Goodness, Winnie,' said Wanda,
looking at the spaceship. 'That *is* modern.
But what are those green things?'

'Oh,' said Winnie. 'Well, they are . . . um
. . . well, aliens . . . to dance for you.'

'Pliggle?' said the aliens.

Wanda and Wayne showed Winnie
around the new bungalow. It was
yawningly tidy and dull.

'The tiles came from Italy, you know.
Wayne's silk cushions came from Iran.
The . . .'

Yawn-yawn! 'Lovely,' said Winnie.
'Now, could we have tea? I'm as parched
as parchment!'

They sat outside on the patio. 'These
chairs came from . . .' nattered on Wanda.
But it didn't matter because Wilbur switched
on some loud music. Winnie slurped
bindweed tea and scoffed raspberry bums
while the aliens began to dance.

Rumpety-tiddly-tump! went

the music.

Poke-poke! went Wilbur with
a wand to make the aliens dance.
Hop-hop! went the aliens.

'Hee hee!' laughed Winnie.

The aliens seemed to enjoy dancing,
and soon even Wanda was clapping along.

'Great tea party, Wanda!' said Winnie
when the dancing was finished.

'Thank you, Winnie!' said Wanda. 'But
don't go just yet, will you? The trouble
with a perfect home is that there's nothing
to do to it.'

70

'Oh you're as bored as an ironing board!' said Winnie. 'Why don't you keep the aliens to keep you busy!' And she shooed them inside, sliding the glass door shut.

'Ooo, mind my ornaments!' said Wanda. But it was too late.

'I'm ever so sorry, Wanda!' said Winnie. 'Quick! Get the aliens back into their spaceship, Wilbur!'

So Wilbur herded them back into their spaceship. **Brrrrm!** The engines fired . . . but the spaceship didn't move.

'That crash landing has broken their navigation system!' said Winnie.

Wilbur pointed to Winnie's sat nav.

'Good thinking, catman!' Winnie. stuck her sat nav onto the spaceship and pressed 'go'. 'They're off!' she said.

'I'll have to redecorate now!' smiled Wanda happily.

'We're off too,' said Winnie. 'Bye!'

'Pling-plip!' said a tiny voice.

'What?' began Winnie.

Wanda blushed. 'I decided to keep just one alien,' she said, lifting her hat. 'It is so stylish, from outer space, you know . . .'

'Bye!' said Winnie. 'Let's see your map then, Wilbur, and find our way home!'

73

Winnie Shapes Up

Snap-snap-snap-snap-snap!

went the alarm croc beside Winnie's bed.

Snip-snap!

'What? Where? Why?' Winnie opened
a bleary eye. *Yawn!* 'It can't be time to get
up already, can it?

Wilbur yawned wide and stretched long.

'Heck, Wilbur!' said Winnie, sitting up.
'I've had a whole night's sleep, so why am
I so sluggy-sloth tired?'

Yawn! went Wilbur.

75

'You're as blooming bad as I am!' said Winnie. 'We should be fitter than this!'

With eyes only half open, stumbling and fumbling, Winnie reached for her clothes. 'I need to get active, and that'll make me healthy. You have to wear special clothes to do that.' Winnie pulled up tracksuit trousers . . . but they got stuck halfway up her legs. 'Heck! It's worse than I thought!' said Winnie. 'I'm as fat as a football! Help me to heave them up, Wilbur!' So Wilbur heaved and Winnie heaved, and the trousers went up, but they were so tight Winnie's legs could hardly bend. 'And the tracksuit top is just as blooming tight!' complained Winnie as she wrenched the zip upwards.

'Me-he-heow!' laughed Wilbur.

'Don't laugh!' said Winnie. 'You're as unfit as I am! We need exercise and healthy food.'

'Meeow!' wailed Wilbur.

'Well, it's no good being too tired to get up in the morning and too fat to fit our clothes,' said Winnie.

So they had just two pong berries each for breakfast. (Although Wilbur gobbled a rat when Winnie wasn't looking.)

Rumble! went Winnie's tummy.
Winnie looked longingly at the biscuit
barrel. 'Chocolate suggestive biscuits!
Tipsy creams!' Then she shook her head.
'No!' she said. 'There isn't any room for
biscuits inside this tracksuit anyway. Off
we go to the gym, Wilbur!'

Gulp! went Wilbur.

There was a personal trainer at the gym. He was big. He was muscly. His name was Nigel.

'Flex your arm!' said Nigel. Winnie bent her flabby arm but it wouldn't flex. 'Bend and stretch!' said Nigel. Winnie bent, but she couldn't bend very far. She tried to stretch, but her tracksuit was so tight she couldn't do that very well either. 'Dear, oh dear,' said Nigel. 'You need a complete workout!'

80

'Me-he-heow!' laughed Wilbur.

'And so does your cat!' said Nigel. 'Go and get dressed in your sporty gear, cat!'

Wilbur came back in a cat tracksuit.

'Tee-hee!' laughed Winnie.

'Flex your arms!' Nigel told Wilbur.

Wilbur did, and—**boing!**—up popped some impressive bulges.

'Wow!' said Winnie. 'I never knew . . .'

'Cut the cackle and get working, Winnie!' said Nigel. 'Wilbur is already in good shape.'

So Wilbur relaxed on a lounger and watched.

'Lift those weights!' said Nigel to Winnie.

Winnie tried. **Heave! Huff-puff!** Wheeze! 'They're too blooming heavy to lift!' she said.

'No excuses!' said Nigel.

But when Nigel turned away for a moment, Winnie whipped out her wand. *'Abracadabra!'*

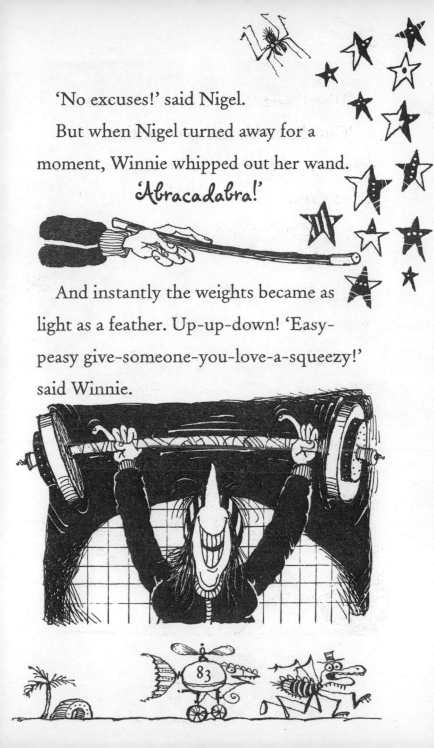

And instantly the weights became as light as a feather. Up-up-down! 'Easy-peasy give-someone-you-love-a-squeezy!' said Winnie.

'Oh! That's better,' said Nigel. He didn't know that Winnie had made all the weights in the gym weightless. They were so light they were starting to lift people up into the air.

'Help!' they called, hovering near the ceiling.

Nigel told Winnie to get on the treadmill.

The treadmill was boring.

'It's just walking!' said Winnie. 'I can do that at home!'

'You should be jogging, not walking!' said Nigel.

'All right, I will!' said Winnie. Out came the wand. *Abracadabra!*

Instantly all the treadmills were going so fast they were just a blur, and people were flying off them backwards.

'Stop!' said Nigel. So Winnie stopped.

'Can I go home now?' she asked.

'No! You're going swimming next,' said Nigel.

There were people already in the pool, splashing about.

'That looks fun!' said Winnie.

'Well, it shouldn't be fun!' said Nigel. 'They should be swimming so fast it hurts!'

'Would you like me to make them go faster?' asked Winnie.

'N—' began Nigel.

But Winnie was already waving her wand. *'Abracadabra!'*

Instantly there was a shark in the pool!
Everyone screamed! And they *did* swim
faster. They swam really, really fast and
then they jumped out of the pool and
they ran!

'There aren't many people left in this gym, are there?' said Winnie. 'Nigel? Nigel?'

But Nigel had run away along with everyone else.

'Just you and me, Wilbur,' said Winnie. 'I'm so hot I feel like an ice cream in an oven. Shall we have a nice cool shower and then go home?'

89

So Winnie unzipped her tracksuit top.
It came off quite easily now. So did the
trousers.

'Ee, I have lost weight!' smiled Winnie.
Then, 'Oh!' she said. Because she was still
wearing something—her woolly pyjamas!
'No blooming wonder the tracksuit was
tight on top of that lot!' said Winnie.
'No flipping wonder I was hot! Silly me!'

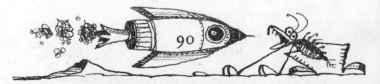

'Me-he-heow!' laughed Wilbur.

'Stop that laughing and take off your tracksuit!' said Winnie.

So Wilbur pulled off his tracksuit . . . and two oranges fell out of the sleeves.

'What?' said Winnie. 'Are those what Nigel thought were your muscles?'

Wilbur grinned.

'You naughty cat!' said Winnie.

As they walked home Winnie had to
hold up her tracksuit trousers to stop them
from falling down.

'I've lost so much weight and without
the pyjamas underneath I'm as skinny as a
skellington! We need to eat, Wilbur!'

'Meeow!' said Wilbur, pointing to a café.

'Good idea!' agreed Winnie.

Winnie and Wilbur ordered everything on the menu. They scoffed and scoffed until they were fit to burst.

And guess who was sitting in the café eating almost as much as they were?

'Nigel!' said Winnie. 'Would you like me to add some sour grape sauce to that lot?' She waved her wand. 'Abr——'

But Nigel was out of the café and running down the street.

'Goodness-pudness, he is keen on his keep fit, isn't he!' said Winnie. 'I don't think I could run with this lot inside me.

In fact I don't think I can . . .' **Rip!**
Winnie's tracksuit trousers split at the
bottom, showing her frilly bloomers.
'Oh, no!' wailed Winnie.

Everyone in the café began laughing and
pointing . . . and soon Winnie *was* running
down the street, after all!

Run to your nearest bookshop
to find these wonderful
Winnie books!

Laura Owen and Korky Paul
Winnie Says Cheese

Laura Owen and Korky Paul
Whizz-Bang Winnie

Laura Owen and Korky Paul
Giddy-Up, Winnie

Laura Owen and Korky Paul
Mini Winnie

Laura Owen and Korky Paul
Winnie the Twit

Laura Owen and Korky Paul
Winnie's Big Catch

Visit

www.winnie-the-witch.com

www.korkypaul.com